* * * THE COBTOWN OBSE[RVER]

TOWN NOTICES:

In case of rain, the dancing will be held at Payne's Tavern. Be sure to bring lanterns as the event will go on 'til pretty late. *

If you are entering any animals or crops to be judged, get them to the Festival by 8:00 A.M. * * *

There will be no drill of the Cobtown Militia this week, show up next Saturday! * * *

THAT'S WHAT THEY SAY!

We are all hoping for good weather for the Harvest Festival. Our neighbors offer these ways of telling what's to come:

* If a donkey's ears are up, it means the weather will be fine. If they take to rubbing against a tree or post, it means rain. So far, my donkeys are all rubbing *and* holding their ears up, so I just can't tell one way or the other.

— Fliberty Jibbert

* You can judge for rain by looking at a chickweed flower. In dry weather, it will open from morn 'til midday. If it closes up tight, the rains will fall.

— Heddy Peggler

* You can tell by the stars. Of course you have to do it at night. You look for the closest star to the moon. If it's on the south side, it means rain. If it is on the north side, it will be clear and windy.

—Jerico Dingle

* If I see my goat, Buckeye, is wet, it's raining. He don't ever bathe.

—Hans Van Ripper

HEDDY PEGGLER

OINKEY

LUCKY HART

JASPER PAYNE

VALENTINE McGINTY

FLIBERTY JIBBERT

THE TWINS

PUMPKINS
FROM THE SKY?
A COBTOWN® STORY
From the Diaries of
Lucky Hart

Written by
JULIA VAN NUTT

Illustrated by
ROBERT VAN NUTT

A Doubleday Book for Young Readers

SISSY DINGLE

MESHACK DINGLE

SHADRACK DINGLE

For Juky, my mama.
J.V.N.

For my mom, who lovingly stitched the Cobtown quilt.
R.V.N.

A DOUBLEDAY BOOK FOR YOUNG READERS
Published by Random House, Inc.
1540 Broadway
New York, New York 10036
Doubleday and the portrayal of an anchor with a dolphin are trademarks of
Random House, Inc.
Text copyright © 1999 by Julia Van Nutt
Illustrations copyright © 1999 by Robert Van Nutt

Cataloging-in-Publication Data is available from the Library of Congress.
ISBN: 0-385-32568-1

The text of this book is set in 15-point Greg.
Book design by Robert Van Nutt

Manufactured in the United States of America
October 1999
10 9 8 7 6 5 4 3 2 1

THE POTATOE ONION?

Dust was flying everywhere, and both Grandma and I were clutching handkerchiefs to our noses and sneezing. We were in her attic looking for an old basket.

Then I saw a stack of old books and a yellow, tattered magazine named The Indiana Farmer and Gardener, March 1845. Inside was advice on raising farm vegetables. As I looked at the names of the vegetables that were discussed, I realized I had never heard of some of them. The magazine mentioned the Polar Plant, Timothy, and the Potatoe Onion.

"Ever eat a potatoe onion?" I asked Grandma. "It sounds delicious."

"Can't say I ever did, but I do remember hearing about them," she said. "Look in my grandma Lucky's old trunk. Try to find her diary about the Cobtown Harvest Festival of 1845."

I dug out the old diary, but I didn't exactly learn about the potatoe onion. No, instead I discovered something that was much more interesting. Pumpkins from the sky?

Wednesday

Now I, Lucky Hart, must tell of the very unusual events that happened today.

Everybody I know is busy getting ready for the Cobtown Harvest Festival. I myself have worked real hard embroidering a picture of my family's house. Nobody would guess a ten-year-old girl made it. It will become part of the Cobtown Quilt.

This morning my aunt Heddy Peggler and her little striped pig, Oinkey, stopped by.

"Come along with Oinkey and me to the Dingles' farm. I need to get some eggs for my baking. If you've finished your quilt panel we'll take it over to show Sissy and her mother," she said.

My friend Sissy Dingle is making her family's quilt picture. When we got to her house she was sitting on the porch working on it.

"Your quilt square looks prettier than mine," I told her. And to me it really did.

"And I think yours is the prettiest one I ever saw."
Sissy laughed. "Mama, come out here and be the judge."

Her mama, Juky Dingle, stepped outside. "What is it?
Why, good morning," she said.

"Which one is prettier?" Sissy and I asked as we held
our panels up for her to see.

Before she could answer, Sissy's two brothers,
Shadrack and Meshack, ran over. "Come look at what
we're entering in the Harvest Festival competition,"
Shadrack said. "We aim to win the Best Vegetable
Contest."

"We're growing a new kind of vegetable, half onion
and half yam," Meshack explained. "We're naming it
Dingle's Onyam! Hurry and see."

The boys took us over to their garden. It didn't look
like much of anything. "Why, that's just a heap of
dirt," I told them.

"Only for now. The onyams are still growing under
the ground," Shadrack said.

"Now, boys, the Harvest Festival is only two days
away," Aunt Heddy said. "Don't you think you'd best dig
one up and see what you've got?"

The brothers looked at each other.

"Miss Peggler's right," Sissy told them. "Let's take a look."

So they started digging. The first thing that came up looked like a wrinkled rag.

"I ain't going to eat that!" Sissy said. "It smells bad."

"Dig up another one," their mama suggested.

The next one looked swollen and had whiskers.

Meshack shook his head and said, "I don't want to eat that one myself."

"We've still got one more," Shadrack said as he dug up his last onyam. It looked like a potato. He threw it on the ground and began to cry.

"It's not all that bad," Sissy said. She grabbed the onyam and started crying.

Then I picked up the onyam and I started crying.

"What's all this?" Heddy asked. She picked it up and, sure enough, tears rolled down her cheeks, but she was laughing, too. "Shadrack, Meshack, you two have made something new, all right, but I'm not sure anybody will want it. What we have here is a sweet potato that makes you cry, like an onion."

"Look! Oinkey's eyes are full of tears," I told them.

Then we all laughed and cried at the same time.

Thursday

There was a frightful storm last night. I could hear things crash and slam outside in the wind. Today our yard is full of broken branches.

I ran up to Aunt Heddy's first thing to see if she and Oinkey had suffered.

She and Oinkey were just heading out her back door when I arrived.

"See anything different up there?" she asked, pointing way uphill toward McGinty's Museum.

"The big old elm tree's gone!" I cried.

"I doubt if it's gone far," she said. "All of my pumpkins are growing behind the McGintys' fence. I bet a few of them got mashed by the fallen elm tree. Let's go take a look."

The three of us climbed up to see the damage.

Old Hans Van Ripper was already staring at the fence. He lives next to it.

"I can't remember a bigger storm than we had last night," he said. "Looks like the old elm is gone for good."

"Oh, my!" Heddy exclaimed. "I can't get into my pumpkin patch. Hans, what can I do? I need to get going on my pumpkin pies for the Harvest Festival Pie-Eating Contest. We also need pumpkins for the Pumpkin Race. And I wanted to enter one in the Best Vegetable Contest. We have to move that tree, and quickly!"

Oinkey looked at Aunt Heddy. Then he shot beneath the tree into the pumpkin patch and turned to see if we were following.

"Oh, nobody but you can scurry under that tree, Oinkey," I told him.

As we started back down the path, we saw the whole McGinty family on the porch of their museum. They, too, were concerned.

"Oh, the tempest wrought its worst! 'Fear not!' I told the family. But alas, behold," the professor said, shaking his head, holding his heart with one hand and waving his handkerchief towards the fallen elm. "We are powerless against the wrath of nature."

He really talks that way!

Aunt Heddy said, "Where's Oinkey? I don't see him." Then she threw her head back, cupped her hands and gave out with one of her pig yodels. That's the way she calls him when he's not in sight. Oinkey poked his snout out of a hole in the bottom of the fence. Then he squeezed through and ran over to us.

"Let's go down to Fliberty Jibbert's place and see if he can help us move the tree," Old Hans suggested.

That's what we did.

"If I thought it would do any good, I'd hitch up my donkeys Muddy and Buddy and try to rig a pulley. But they aren't strong enough for that big old elm. The tree will have to be chopped up into pieces. That will take several days," Fliberty told her. "We cannot get all those pumpkins out in time for the fair. I know that's disappointing." Oinkey pushed up against Aunt Heddy to let her know he was feeling bad, too.

She kneeled down to him. "Oinkey, we will have to think of some way to get those pumpkins," she said. "Cobtown has never held a Harvest Festival without a Peggler's Pumpkin Race. There must be something we can do." She and Oinkey started back towards their home.

Old Hans, Fliberty and I didn't say a word, but we all felt bad.

Tomorrow is the last day before the Harvest Festival.

Will there be any ???

FUN & GAMES!

Friday

I went over to the Beaver Meadow this morning. The place was bustling with folks getting ready for tomorrow's Cobtown Harvest Festival.

"See here, if we don't have any pumpkins, then we can't have the Pumpkin Race. But there's other things just as good, like weaving straw or bobbing for apples," Fliberty told all the children of Cobtown as we gathered around him. He was making the frame for hanging the Cobtown Quilt.

"Pshaw! I don't think straw weaving is just as good," whined Valentine McGinty. "I'm entering the Pie-Eating Contest, and the whole point is to eat the most pumpkin pies. Why, I couldn't get down half as many if they were just plain old apple pies."

Just then the Ravenell Twins came loping past. They had two of their legs tied together and were trying to run. "We're getting ready for the Three-Legged Race," they panted.

"And here we just thought you were acting natural," Valentine said, sniggering.

Jasper Payne's Weather Predictor

Hang it outside on a nail.

If it's wet —— it's raining.
If it's white —— it's snowing.
If it's stiff —— it's freezing.
If it's moving —— it's windy.
If it's gone —— it's been stolen!

Patented by —— J. Payne 1845

"Valentine, don't be so rude," I warned him. "Everybody is sorry about Aunt Heddy's pumpkins, especially her. Look, there's your father, setting up his table of Vegetable Oddities. There's Apple Jack setting up his cider booth and Miss Lilly Fields putting the final stitches in the Cobtown Quilt. Everybody's got something to do. But where's Aunt Heddy? She's home feeling bad and useless because of that old elm tree falling over."

Fliberty stopped hammering and said, "Jasper Payne, quit that whistling. It's getting on my nerves."

"I've got to practice, Fliberty, that's the only way I can beat Virgil Squib in the Whistling Contest tomorrow."

"Then do it somewhere else, or, better yet, why don't you all pay Heddy a visit and see how she's doing?" Fliberty went back to his hammering.

Well, we obeyed. Heddy was looking queer, though. She was sitting on her back porch just staring towards her pumpkin patch. Oinkey was acting funny, too. He kept running halfway up the hill, then turning and giving a loud "Oink." Then he'd run back down, stare at us and oink again.

"Aunt Heddy, want to go with us over to the Dingles' farm?" I asked.

"Dingles'? No, I don't want to go anywhere. Jasper Payne, stop that terrible whistling. You'll drive us to distraction."

I've never seen her or Oinkey behave like that.

Over at the Dingles' there was a bustle of activity. Juky Dingle was telling everybody what to do as she and Sissy cooked yams.

"Lucky, even though you witnessed an onyam crop failure the other day, there's still going to be Dingle's Onyams at the Harvest Festival," Sissy said to me. "We're setting up our own booth. Mama said we had us a stroke of genius in inventing the Onyam. Trouble is, we couldn't get an onion and a yam to grow together. But Mama says we can <u>cook</u> them together. We are making yam patties and putting a little bit of onion jam in the center. At the festival, we'll brown the patties fresh on the spot. Dingle's Onyams, why, there's nothing ever tasted better," Sissy said as she put more wood on the fire.

I will eat one tomorrow at the fair. Maybe I will eat two.

Saturday

Today brought a big surprise. I woke up thinking of the good music and food and contests and fun I would have with all my friends. Then I remembered Aunt Heddy and the way she was acting yesterday. "I better bring her down here to spend the day," I thought.

Imagine my surprise when I got to her house and found a blazing fire in the hearth. Aunt Heddy was singing and making pie crusts. Oinkey was right next to her, looking excited. "Are you going to make apple pies?" I asked her.

She laughed, threw open her back door and said, "Look at the miracle." There, piled up all over her back yard, were more pumpkins than I could count.

"How did they get here?" I asked, not believing my eyes.

"Oinkey woke me up at first light. He kept bumping into the bed so as to shake me awake. Then he started going 'Oink!' right in my ear. When I stood up, he ran out the door and I followed. I was amazed! This house was surrounded by my pumpkins. It was as if the entire crop had moved itself over the fence and the elm tree, too. But look here, Lucky, roll up your sleeves and help me get these pies ready for the Pie-Eating Contest."

Just then, Old Hans came up to the back door. "What's all this, Heddy? How on earth did you get your pumpkins around that elm tree?" he asked.

"We were wondering the same, Hans. Nobody saw a thing as far as I know," Aunt Heddy told him.

"I heard some odd sounds last night, I did," Old Hans said. "A rumbling kept passing my door. I got up to take a look several times, but it was too dark to see anything. I slept poorly, though, I can attest to that."

Then Professor McGinty and his whole family stopped by. "My dear Miss Peggler, correct me if I'm wrong," the Professor said, "but we have here a supernatural event. These pumpkins have moved themselves by defying gravity. I have read of instances where strange objects have fallen to the earth. Why, I believe it has rained pumpkins. Yes, behold, pumpkins from the sky, I say."

"It could be, Cornelius," Aunt Heddy said, "but I've got so much work to do that I can't waste time speculating. These pumpkins have arrived and I'm cooking them. That's all I know for sure."

Everybody in town made a point to stop by and went away scratching their heads. Nobody could figure it.

HARVEST FESTIVAL!

We baked the pies and took them down to the Beaver Meadow. Everything looked exciting! The Cobtown Quilt was waving in the breeze, and I could see my family's panel, which said "Hart." It looked especially beautiful.

They were just starting the Whistling Contest, and only two folks were entered to compete. Jasper was one. Virgil Squib, town poet, who works for the rail-road, was the other. Jasper whistled "Yankee Doodle" and did a beautiful job. All his bothersome practicing had paid off. Then Virgil surprised everybody by whistling like a mocking-bird. He didn't carry any tune but tweeted like every bird we knew. The judges decided that they both had won.

Sissy and her family had a big crowd around their cooking booth. "Dingle's Onyams" was written on their banner. Folks were saying that they couldn't get enough of them. I felt the same way. One bite and I wanted more. So did Mama and Papa. Now onyams are my favorite food. And you can only get them here in Cobtown.

We had fiddle music by Jerico Dingle, and Jasper played along on his spoons and even whistled a part now and then. Everything was so delightful, but the most exciting event of all was the Pumpkin Race.

The race course starts up behind Aunt Heddy's house and turns back at Ravenell's Store. The finish line is right in front of The Cobtown Observer. The idea is to choose a pumpkin and when Fliberty says "Go!" roll it across the finish line first. It's not easy.

The Ravenell Twins took one pumpkin between them. One pushed while the other stayed out front to keep it on the path. Jasper chose a speedy-looking little pumpkin and left the twins behind. Valentine tried to roll the largest one but didn't get far. He had just won the Pie-Eating Contest and wasn't up to running.

But here comes the surprise.

Just as Jasper's tumbler rounded the curve, a speeding shape shot out from under a bush. It intercepted the spinning pumpkin and pushed it past the finish line and over into Aunt Heddy's front yard! It was Oinkey! He didn't slow down, either, but turned back and caught the Ravenells' pumpkin and quickly pushed it, too, into Aunt Heddy's yard. Then he scurried back and took Valentine's away from him. Everyone cheered as he herded that big one right across the finish line and up to Aunt Heddy's yard.

Then the crowd fell silent. What had we just seen? Could it be that the pumpkins did not fly over the McGintys' fence but were pushed out through a hole underneath it? Were the pumpkins rolled to their rightful owner by a pig? Nobody really knew for sure, but we did know one thing. Oinkey had won the Pumpkin Race.

Aunt Heddy accepted the winning ribbon for him. She tied it around Oinkey's neck and he strutted back and forth in front of the Cobtown Quilt. I guess he felt mighty proud. And so did I.

Now I'm wondering if he can whistle. I'm sure nobody has asked him to try. If he can, well, next year he just might win another first-prize ribbon. I always say he's as good a pig as you would ever want to know.

All of this really happened at the Cobtown Harvest Festival, 1845.

* Lucky Hart *
1845.
*

COBTOWN

HARVEST FESTIVAL

ANIMALS,
FRUITS,
VEGETABLES,
POULTRY.

PIES! GAMES! PRIZES! CIDER!

FUN FOR ALL!

AT THE BEAVER MEADOW,
COBTOWN

THE COBTOWN OBSERVER

I.B. HOOTIE: CHIEF CORRESPONDENT, EDITOR, PRINTER AND PUBLISHER.

COBTOWN, BETTER GET YOUR BEASTS & VEGETABLES READY FOR THE HARVEST FESTIVAL!

Well, neighbors, it looks like it's that time of year again! The leaves have all turned color, the cool weather is here, and the crops are in. That can mean only one thing: it's time for the Harvest Festival! We expect the Beaver Meadow to be pretty crowded on Saturday what with you folks bringing your best to show. There will be tents for judging the finest animals, best vegetables, and your most delicious baked goods. The McGintys are planning to have a Vegetable Oddities competition, so bring all your double-headed gourds and curiously shaped carrots. You could be a winner! ✳

FUN & GAMES!

I'll wager there is a whole lot of activity in your kitchens these days. "We've had to order extra flour and spice sales have been brisk," Mary Ravenell told us at the General Store. This probably means we will have a Pie Eating Contest to remember! We know of some children (and adults) who can hardly wait for this event! For the quick and nimble among us, there will be a three-legged race. A Whistling Contest has been added to this year's games, so pucker up. As always, the Pumpkin Rolling Race will be the last event. Heddy Peggler promises us a good crop to choose from.

✳ ✳ ✳ ✳ ✳ ✳ ✳ ✳

SEE THE NEW COBTOWN QUILT!

We are all looking forward to seeing the new town quilt. For the past year the skilled fingers of our ladies and daughters have been busy with needle and thread in the creation of a cloth masterpiece! The quilt is made up of nine squares. Each one shows a house and is labeled with the name of the family who lives there. Miss Lilly Fields was in charge of the project and will assemble the quilt in time to show it at the Harvest Festival. We can all take pride in this work of love! ✳

MUSIC & DANCE

Don't forget to bring your dancin' shoes! There's going to be a bonfire this Saturday night with dancing to the music of Jerico Dingle's fiddle! Who could ask for more in one day! ✳ ✳ ✳ ✳